Ducky
Diary Three

**Other books by
Ann M. Martin**

Leo the Magnificat
Rachel Parker, Kindergarten Show-off
Eleven Kids, One Summer
Ma and Pa Dracula
Yours Turly, Shirley
Ten Kids, No Pets
Slam Book
Just a Summer Romance
Missing Since Monday
With You and Without You
Me and Katie (the Pest)
Stage Fright
Inside Out
Bummer Summer

THE KIDS IN MS. COLMAN'S CLASS series
BABY-SITTERS LITTLE SISTER series
THE BABY-SITTERS CLUB mysteries
THE BABY-SITTERS CLUB series
CALIFORNIA DIARIES series

written with Paula Danziger:
Snail Mail No More
P.S. Longer Letter Later

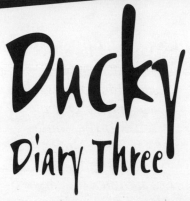

California Diaries #15

Ducky
Diary Three

Ann M. Martin

SCHOLASTIC INC.
New York Toronto London Auckland Sydney
Mexico City New Delhi Hong Kong

The author gratefully acknowledges
Nola Thacker
for her help in
preparing this manuscript.

ISBN 0-439-09549-2

12 11 10 9 8 7 6 5 4 3 2 1   0/0 1 2 3 4 5/0

Printed in the U.S.A.   40
First Scholastic printing, September 2000

Aug. 15
Work. Work. Work.
Or,
The True Story of Ducky

You're complaining about work.

Work is good. Work is not being at home counting the half-full (half-empty) cereal boxes that line the counters of our kitchen.

Cereal boxes are a big decorating item in your house since Ted has suddenly decided to eat most of his meals at the college caf. This is so he doesn't have to wash dishes.

Lately, Ted seems to feel overextended when he has to rinse out a cereal bowl and load it into the dishwasher.

You believe, almost, that if you had a dog, Ted would put all plates and utensils down for the dog to lick clean. Then . . .

No. You malign him, Ducky.

He wouldn't really put them back on the shelf.

He'd just stack them in the sink.

But enough about Ted. Enough about life on the take-out menu.

Let's talk about...

You.

Me.

Work.

Work is BEING IN CHARGE.

Okay. So you're not in charge of the bookstore exactly. But Mr. W is out at the moment and only you and Sunny are here.

Process of elimination: Boss gone.

Person (or persons) in charge: Sunny (boss's daughter). and/or Ducky.

No, let's call you CHRISTOPHER for the mo. Sounds more bosslike.

Christopher. (Boss's daughter's best friend.)

Are you? Are you, Christopher "Ducky" McCrae, the BF of Sunny Winslow?

Too much. You don't need the pressure of figuring it out. Why define something that doesn't need defining?

Why overanalyze EVERYTHING?

Okay. The boss's daughter is your very good, close personal friend. You feel comfortable with that.

Right now Sunny is organizing the impulse purchases around the cash register — all the little, cute, not-too-high-ticket items that you can point out

TO CUSTOMERS AS YOU RING UP THEIR PURCHASES. OR IF THEY ARE TRULY GOOD CUSTOMERS, THEY PICK 'EM UP THEMSELVES AND SAY, "THIS IS SOOO CUTE," AND TOSS 'EM IN WITH THE OTHER BOOKS.

YOU DO NOT THINK LITTLE TINY BOOKS ARE CUTE.

YOU HAVE (TRUE CONFESSIONS) NEVER USED A BOOKMARK IN YOUR LIFE. SEASONALLY THEMED PENS — THE KIND WITH DRACULA PAINTED ON THEM OR WHATEVER — ARE NOT A FASHION STATEMENT, IN YOUR OPINION.

BUT HEY, WHATEVER.

SUNNY LOOKS UP, SEES YOU LOOKING, AND SMILES.

SHE KNOWS HOW YOU FEEL ABOUT THE IMPULSE ITEMS.

SHE HERSELF LIKES THEM.

A STRONG WOMAN WITH A MIND OF HER OWN.

INCOMING CUSTOMER.

D: MAY I HELP YOU?

IC: NO. THANKS.

D: WELL, LET ME KNOW IF I CAN.

IC: RIGHT.

SUNNY PASSES YOU WITH A BIG BOX. SHE PUTS IT DOWN NEXT TO THE FRONT DISPLAY WINDOW AND OPENS IT. SHE PEERS IN.

You peer in.

You get a shock.

It is full of Barbie dolls.

"Sunny," you say, "we have to talk."

Ignoring you, she says, "There's a bucket of sand by the back door. Would you get that for me?"

You obey.

When you return, Sunny is emptying all the best-sellers from the window.

You return them to the shelves, refraining from asking questions. By now, you have cleverly deduced that Sunny has PLANS for these dolls. Plans involving the window display.

You spend a pleasant half hour or so pulling books that involve beaches, oceans, and summer activities from the shelves. These include a horror book set at the beach, Moby-Dick, several guides to shells, a book about beach vacations, and Treasure Island (personal childhood favorite). You've decided to insist it be included, even if Sunny objects.

But she doesn't. Instead, she suggests that you get some petty cash and buy a bottle of suntan lotion and some not-too-uncool-but-cheap sunglasses to go with the display.

You return to find Sunny arranging the books on a couple of beach towels that she has also brought along.

You remind her that she'll be in trouble if she gets sand in the books' bindings.

Or at least if they were library books she would be.

She makes a face. You make a face back.

You know from humiliating childhood experience leading to lifelong fear of the species Librarianimus horribilus.

Also lions, tigers, bears.

Cro Mags?

You will not think about those jerks, those hall jockeys, those losers who somehow manage to make your life miserable.

School is out. For the summer.

You have no fear.

No fear. Ducky fears no Cro Mag. Nor Neanderthal either. (Neither?)

Movie advertisement:

Ducky is John Wayne. And the Duke fears NO MAN.

But did John "the Duke" Wayne fear women? Did he . . .

Another customer.

MOMENTS LATER

ANOTHER CUSTOMER WHO POLITELY DECLINES YOUR OFFER OF ASSISTANCE.

YOU TRY NOT TO FEEL REJECTED.

OKAY, JUST KIDDING. CUSTOMER REJECTION HAPPENS NOT TO BE A PROBLEM FOR ...

WHAT IS SUNNY MAKING THOSE FACES FOR? WHY IS SHE POINTING AT THAT CUSTOMER? YEAH, THE BAGGY CLOTHES ARE A BIT FASHION-OVER BUT ...

A JOHN WAYNE MOMENT

YOU LOOK UP. SEE THE GUY SLIDE A VERY LARGE ART BOOK INTO THE INNER POCKET OF HIS COAT.

YOU BLINK. NOT A DUKE BLINK, A DUCK BLINK.

YOU DO NOT BELIEVE YOUR EYES.

THE GUY STARTS TO WALK OH-SO-CASUALLY TO THE DOOR.

SUNNY SLIDES IN FRONT. "DID YOU FIND EVERYTHING YOU NEEDED?" SHE ASKS.

HER EYES ARE SENDING YOU SIGNALS.

DIAL 911?

NO.

Call the police the regular way?

No.

"No," says the shoplifter. He steps to one side.

Sunny steps to the same side.

He steps to the other side.

Sunny steps to the other side.

A shoplifter dance.

You recover your (dim) wits and race (casually, sweating, dry-mouthed) to join the party. "Hey," you say.

(Hey? _Hey?_ The Duke, wherever he is, is NOT impressed.)

"I think you might have forgotten to pay for something."

The guy, now that you notice, is big. As in MUCH TALLER THAN YOU.

He's also armed with a large, heavy art book.

You brace yourself for the possible direct delivery of art appreciation to your skull. You smile.

Sunny opens her mouth. You glance at her and beam the following universal signal to her: BE PREPARED. FOR ANYTHING.

Does she understand it?

She frowns slightly, closes her mouth. Her look says, YOUR TURN.

"What?" says the guy. "What are you talking

ABOUT?" HE IS PRETTY CONVINCING. YOU ARE AMAZED AT HOW CONVINCING HE IS. YOU WANT TO BELIEVE HIM.

AND THEN HE DOES THE MOST AMAZINGLY GUILTY THING IN THE WORLD. HE PUTS HIS HAND OVER THE INSIDE POCKET WHERE THE BOOK IS STASHED (OR BOOKS — AT THAT MOMENT, YOU DON'T KNOW HOW MANY HE'S GOT KANGAROOED AWAY IN HIDDEN POUCHES).

YOU LOOK AT HIS HAND.

YOU LOOK UP AT HIM.

YOU FOLD YOUR ARMS AND RAISE ONE EYEBROW.

YOU ADMIT, HERE ONLY, THAT YOU'VE PRACTICED THIS LOOK ON OCCASION. PRIVATELY. BUT YOU HAVE NEVER, EVER SAID, "BOND. JAMES BOND" WHILE DOING IT.

EVER.

YOU STARE AT MR. POCKET BOOK. HE STARES AT YOU.

IT GETS WAY TOO QUIET. A LITTLE PULSE IS JUMPING AT ONE CORNER OF HIS MOUTH. HE NEEDS A SHAVE. BUT NOT MUCH. HIS FACE IS MOSTLY FUZZY AND YOU REALIZE THAT HE IS YOUNGER THAN YOU THOUGHT HE WAS.

THEN SUNNY SAYS, "IT HAPPENS MORE THAN YOU'D THINK. BOOK PEOPLE ARE SO ABSENTMINDED. AND THEY LEAVE THINGS HERE ALL THE TIME TOO. CAR KEYS. GLOVES. WE HAVE QUITE A LOST-AND-FOUND COLLECTION.... ANYWAY, IF YOU'LL STEP TO THE REGISTER, I'LL BE GLAD TO RING UP YOUR CHOICES FOR YOU."

Pocket Book looks at you.

You drop the eyebrow and give him an encouraging nod.

"Right," he says.

You step aside and motion toward the register. Sunny stays beside him and you step in to guard the rear as she moves around to ring up his purchases.

"Check?" he croaks. "Is a check okay?"

"Cash," Sunny says smoothly. "We prefer cash."

Like she's going to take a check from him. Like he's gonna use his REAL checkbook.

Okay, so maybe he would. Who knows?

He fumbles out a wallet — and the art book.

You have an inspired moment and say, "You might want to make sure you haven't forgotten any other books you were interested in buying."

He jumps. His hand goes to the other side of his coat.

You hope this guy doesn't make a living doing this. Apart from the illegality thing, the ripping-people-off-who-are-trying-to-make-a-living-themselves thing, he's gonna starve.

He's really bad at his job.

He ends up paying for three paperbacks, but

NOT THE ART BOOK. Not enough of the folding green stuff.

And Sunny tells him, with deeply insincere regret, that the credit card machine is not working.

Just in case his credit cards are faux. Smooth Sunny.

The shoplifter bolts with his purchases.

You and Sunny face each other.

CUT TO:

Sunny: You were cool, Ducky. I mean, I was totally freaked and there you were.

D: Hey [there's that word again], if you hadn't stepped in front of him, he would've been so gone.

S: Yeah, but after I did that, I didn't know what to do.

D: That line about book people being absentminded? Brilliant.

S [modestly]: Thank you. My hero.

D: My hero.

Sunny laughs. You laugh.

"We're a good team," Sunny says.

"Yeah," you say. "We are."

Aug. 16

Okay. You're a sixteen-year-old boy and you like to go shopping. You just spent the day shopping.

With a girl.

Who is thirteen.

(But not just any girl. Sunny.)

Does this make you strange?

Answer: No. You are already strange.

Besides, who cares? It's not like anyone saw you. And even if they did, WHY DO YOU CARE?

And besides again, even if THEY (whoever they are) saw you, they'd just think you were hanging out with a cute girl.

Anyway, it wasn't your idea to go shopping. Sunny and you were hanging at the mall and it just . . . happened.

One minute you were watching the little kids throw pennies in the fountain (standing, of course, right next to the sign that said, "Please don't throw pennies in the fountain"). The next minute, you found yourself giving face time to window displays. Nodding when Sunny said, "Puh-lease, the colors are unnatural. In a bad way."

Remarking on, for example, your need, someday, for something in cashmere.

"I wouldn't have to wear it," you say. "Just keep it around and pet it. A cashmere pet. Soft. Color-coordinated. House-trained."

Sunny is laughing.

And then wham, bam, you're in a store.

Actually, you go willingly into your favorite try-on-and-spend emporium. Lots of retro stuff. Sunny has a sunglasses vision (that's what she calls it) and you end up with a pair of either extremely geeky or over-the-edge-cool old sunglasses that she insists you wear even though you are indoors.

"It's a very bright mall," she says.

"Tell me before I walk into, say, a display. Or a store window," you reply.

You drift into a wig place. You're a little creeped out by it. All those loose scalps on all those severed heads.

But Sunny dives right in, trying on wigs like they're hats.

A black Cher number with bangs — not Sunny's best look.

Not yours either.

Even with the dark glasses.

The "wig consultant" has been offering advice to

another "client." She makes the sale, the client bags the hair, and then the consultant turns to you and Sunny.

Sunny is now in a Little Orphan Annie number: red curls going SPROING!

The consultant gives her a mouthful of smile. "May I help you?" she says.

Unspoken words: "Like, out of my store? Now?"

"No thanks." Sunny picks up a mirror to get a better peek at the back of her head.

"Orphan Annie isn't your style," you say and want to BITE OFF YOUR TONGUE since it has been — what? — only a few months since Mrs. Winslow died.

"Half an orphan might be," Sunny says without missing a beat.

Her eyes meet yours in the mirror. They have a funny expression. Challenging? Expectant?

You answer with a disgusted face.

You never know what Sunny's going to say. It's one of the things you like about her.

You also like that you can let her know when you think she's pushing 'tude on you.

The look vanishes from Sunny's eyes. She smiles. Megawatt. Indecipherable.

Like you've passed a test.

She says, "Don't wig on me, Ducky."

The consultant's teeth disappear into a thin-lipped, "been there, heard that" grimace.

You ponder the meaning of Sunny's look, her smile.

You ponder the idea that selling wigs is sort of like selling shoes, only at the other end.

Sunny removes the red fright curls. She stares at herself for a second in the mirror, smooths her own much-better-looking hair, and says, "Do you think I'm pretty, Ducky?"

This you didn't expect.

You say, "Pretty?" in a cowardly, stalling-for-time sort of way. You look at the wig. You look at Sunny.

You realize she is pretty. Without a doubt.

"As in not ugly," says Sunny.

Are you in trouble? Could be. Trying to keep it light you say, "Without the wig you are beautiful."

Sunny looks pleased and you try not to look relieved when she laughs. You laugh too.

Inside you are going, "WHEWWWWW!"

What if Sunny had asked you that (sorry to be sexist but so far you've never heard a guy ask this) GIRL QUESTION: "Do I look fat?"

No right answer to that one.

And what does it mean, anyway?

Fat compared to what?

Fat, how?

Fatheaded, if you're a Cro Mag?

Define fat.

Fat in which places?

Fat according to what culture?

Sunny flutters her eyelashes at you, gives the rest of the wigs a quick look, then says thanks to the consultant.

We wander out of the wig store and loiter/saunter around the mall.

Sunny catches your hand and swings it gleefully.

"Isn't this fun?" she says.

"It is," you say back.

"Next time we go out to play, you get to choose the game."

"Mall hunt is a pretty good one."

"Quality time," Sunny agrees. "You know, Ducky, you are SO not like other guys."

Is this a good thing? A bad thing?

It's not a thing you didn't know already, thanks to the Cro Mags.

You wonder if this is Sunny's way of saying, "You're weird, Ducky, but it's okay."

You say, "Yeah, but am I pretty?"

That sets Sunny off. She is still snorting with laughter as you pass the food court.

You are wondering if you are, well, ugly. You meant to be funny, but did Sunny have to laugh quite so hard?

You nod absently as Sunny finally stops laughing, sniffs, and pronounces the odor "Mystery Meat."

"We'd have to give Dawn artificial resuscitation," she remarks.

"It's pretty rank," you say. "A smell like that makes you understand Dawn's eco-vegetarian ways."

"True," Sunny agrees.

You remember Dawn is in Connecticut for the summer with her mom and stepfather, etc. You ponder the fact that Dawn goes back and forth between two sets of parents while your parents just go away.

To places like Greece. Crete, to be specific.

Why Crete?

Why not Crete? It's far away. Your parents seem to like that.

A toy store display catches Sunny's eye. "Look," she says. "Noah's Ark. All the animals two by two going up into the boat."

You squint through the dark glasses.

"Like everyone we know," says Sunny. "Two by two."

"On cruises?" you say.

She ignores your lame humor. "Amalia and

Brendan, who've been together much since Brendan got back from camp. Tyler...

"Maggie says he's not her boyfriend—" you begin.

"Maggie's just talking. They _are_ girlfriend-boyfriend. Look at how they're acting. Togetherness Plus while Tyler's in town between movies."

"I guess," you say. "I haven't seen that much of them."

"'Cause they're seeing soooo much of each other," Sunny says triumphantly.

"I'm glad. For Maggie. And for Tyler."

"Yeah. Me too."

Sunny sits on a bench, pats the seat beside her.

"Ah, nature," you say, pushing aside the fronds of the tree above the bench. It's one of those mall trees that need no light.

Originally from the jungle?

"What we need here are some artificial pigeons to feed," you remark.

You turn to see Sunny staring. At you.

That look again.

Is something going on in Sunny's life that she's not telling you? Should you ask?

"Sunny?" you say.

She blinks. "Sorry. Spacing."

She smiles at you.

You smile at her.

The tree rustles in... who knows what? The mall breeze? The fumes from the food court?

A real mall moment.

Aug. 20
Friday
Friends (a NOT-for-Television Story)

Ring, ring.

Ducky picks up the phone.

MOTHER OF DUCKY: Christopher. Darling, how are you?

D: Fine. Cooking dinner.

MOD: How nice! [Pause] Cooking? Dinner?

D: Yes. How are you? How's Crete?

MOD: I guess it's dinnertime, isn't it?

D: Here. What time is it there?

MOD: Your father says hello. Do you want to talk to him?

D: Tell him hello. I'm making fruit salad. So we don't get scurvy.

MOD: [Pause] Oh. Is Ted there?

D: Hold on. TED!

World-traveling parents do that. They call and ask questions and you answer and you have a conversation in which you talk about one thing and they talk about another. Maybe it's the difference in time zones.

Maybe as long as they hear the voices of their sons, they figure everything is okay.

It's okay. If you like having a Ted-sized family.

You might say you still have issues with them for NOT BEING HERE, especially for the basic family moments: Christmas, for example.

But you don't really have issues, do you, Ducky? Hardly at all. You like your freedom. You are learning important life skills.

Housecleaning. Ordering takeout.

Cooking.

You wonder if you will be a chef. You've learned to cook in self-defense.

You cook because a man (even John "the Duck" Wayne) cannot live on cereal and take-out pizza alone.

Of course, your brother scarfs it up and says, "Decent," and then LEAVES the dishes. You say, "Ted, I cooked. You clean up."

He says, "Sure. Later."

"Later" in Ted-speak means "before the parents get home."

Weeks. Months. Years.

Well, maybe not years.

So you sigh your long-suffering sigh, reject the thought of dumping the remainder of the fruit salad over your ungrateful slob of a brother's head, remind yourself he's the only bro you have, and clean up yourself.

In self-defense. Another course not offered in the local dojo: housework as self-defense.

Ah, domestic arts.

Maybe that's why your parents travel. No housework.

They pack. They unpack. When they get to a big enough hotel, they call room service and have everything cleaned.

Your father is talking about going to Pompeii, in Italy.

You mention that you thought Pompeii was buried under ash or something.

"You know about Pompeii?" Your mother sounds surprised and pleased.

You almost tell her you watched a late-night TV movie about it, but you stop.

Both the words "late night" and "TV" make parents go, well, parental.

You say, "Mmm."

"Fascinating place," she says. "An entire town buried in volcanic ash."

You imagine your own house buried in volcanic ash. When they dug it up in the future, what would they think?

LATER

Busy week. Haven't had much time.

Time flies. Doesn't matter if you're having fun or just cooking and cleaning and having nonconversations with your long-distance parents.

Big zero night ahead.

Phone.

Okay, back.

Just when you thought you could count on a quiet, boring evening at home.

Dawn is back. Sunny just called to tell you. Plus

Tyler has returned to NYC. He's in a play. Being in a play on Broadway gives him more acting experience, Sunny says.

Sunny wants all the friends to get together for fun.

Tonight.

See you. Later.

Post Friends and Fun

Liked the movie. Liked the food. Liked the company.

But wouldn't you know it, all is not perfect in Ducky Land.

Are you the only one who notices these things? The only one who feels the urge, the need to smooth it all over? The only one who wonders if he is imagining it all? Being hypersensitive?

In the course of friends' night out you discover (or learn more about) Maggie's Absent Without Leave status.

Your parents are AWOL physically.

So is Maggie's father. (In Vancouver, working on a movie deal.)

Her mom, however, is home, but absent. She spends her time drinking.

Maggie has faced down an eating disorder. She sees a therapist. She is strong and getting stronger.

She is tough and brave and cool, and you admire her for it.

But you are taken aback at the diner post-flick when Maggie says, flatly, "My mom was loaded when I left. If I'm lucky, when I get home tonight she'll be passed out and I won't have to deal with her."

This stops the conversation pretty much cold.

Maggie says, "She might as well not be there. If it weren't for Pilar, the house would fall down around our ears."

Amalia gives Maggie a quick sympathetic look and says, "Stay over at my house tonight, Maggie. You know you always can."

Maggie ducks her head. "Enough. I've stayed over enough this week."

Sunny offers her house too. Maggie says, "Thanks. I'll keep you in mind if it's too reeking at home. Plus, Zeke needs me." Her voice is bitter. Defeated.

You decide to change the subject. You say, brilliantly, "So, what is everybody going to have to eat?"

But it works. You plunge into a deep discussion of the menu. You can't help but be relieved that Maggie

DIVES RIGHT INTO THE SUBJECT TOO. YOU ALSO HOPE, ONCE MORE, THAT NO ONE NOTICES YOUR RELIEF. YOU DON'T WANT MAGGIE TO THINK YOU'RE THINKING ABOUT HER RECENT EATING PROBLEMS.

EVEN IF YOU ARE.

YOU ALL ORDER MASSIVE AMOUNTS OF FOOD. YOU HOLD YOUR STRAW UNDER YOUR NOSE AND DO REVIEWS OF THE GREEN SALAD, THE BURGERS, THE FRIES, EVEN THE SODA. "FIZZY, BUT WITH A SUBTLE BOUQUET SUGGESTIVE OF SPORTING EVENTS AND MOVIE THEATERS," YOU SAY.

YOU ARE EMBARRASSINGLY PLEASED WHEN EVERYONE LAUGHS.

SUNNY SAYS, "I BET YOU HAVE A LOT MORE HIDDEN TALENTS, DUCKY." SHE IS LEANING AGAINST YOU.

YOU PUT ON A FAKE FRENCH ACCENT AND SAY, "YES. I SPEAK ZEVERAL LANGUAGES TOO, INCLUDING ZE LANGUAGE OF LUV."

EVERYONE CRACKS UP.

EXCEPT SUNNY. SHE USUALLY LAUGHS THE HARDEST AT YOUR JOKES, ESPECIALLY LATELY. BUT NOW SHE JUST LOOKS AT YOU.

WHY DO YOU SUDDENLY WISH YOU HAD THOSE DARK GLASSES AGAIN?

YOU THINK OF SUNNY AS BEING ON PRETTY MUCH THE SAME PAGE AS YOU, BUT AT THE MOMENT, YOU FEEL LIKE

she's reading from another book altogether. You
don't get what the look means.

You smile and glance away and see Dawn and
Brendan looking at you too.

They look at Sunny. They look at you.

They exchange glances.

You become busy with the soda and decide to leave
the jokes to other people for awhile.

After all, you don't have to entertain everyone
else ALL the time, do you, Ducky?

It's not your JOB.

Feeling self-conscious and stupid, you focus on
making normal, low-key conversation.

Only now Sunny is laughing at everything you say.
Or at least smiling.

How do you take this?

Is Sunny in ONE OF HER MOODS?

You decide to be cool. You concentrate on the
others at the table, listening to them, not saying
much.

You notice things.

One of the things you notice is when Brendan puts
his hand over Amalia's on the table, she slides her
hand away.

When Brendan drapes his arm casually over the back of the booth (and her shoulders), she jumps up.

"'Scuse me," she says.

Dawn, Maggie, and Sunny immediately jump up too.

They all go to the bathroom.

It's a girl thing.

Brendan and you look at each other but you don't comment on it. Instead, Brendan says something about the A's and you say something about the Dodgers.

Fortunately, the girls don't stay away too long. You can only discuss so much baseball.

But Ted keeps you up to speed on it, since it's what guys talk to each other about instead of about, well, the things girls talk about.

Don't know why.

It's a guy thing.

Late.

Later.

Aug. 21
Guy Things. Friends.

I'm not very good at guy things. And I just don't get it. It's like all the other guys have this book of rules that someone forgot to give me.

Or maybe I got the book, but some of the pages were left out.

Or maybe I got a different book? Is there more than one book of how to be a guy?

Like, guys are supposed to be cool. Not too emotional. Bored with girl things. Shopping is stopping on the street to admire a set of wheels. Or a retrofitted Harley, maybe. Cooking is what you do with a microwave and a frozen pizza.

Guys watch sports on television. They play sports. They talk about "chicks" and "babes." The gross, loser Cro Mags can get pretty graphic about it, thinking (pathetically) they're being superstuds.

Not all guys are like that, of course. But most sort of fit along the spectrum. At one end are Cro Mags and in the middle are ordinary guys and . . .

What am I?

Am I a failed guy? So young?

Wait a minute: Just because I'm not IN LOVE with Sunny doesn't make me a failure. And there are plenty of guys who cook (aka RICH AND FAMOUS CHEFS) and like cool clothes (ROCK STARS, MOVIE GUYS).

Still, if I understood this whole guy thing, would I feel so freaked out about Sunny?

I work in a bookstore. Where on the shelves is the book on how to be a GUY?????

YOU LISTEN TO A LAME-O JOKE FOR THE ONE THOUSANDTH TIME: HI, READ ANY GOOD BOOKS LATELY?

YOU SMILE AT THE LAME-O CUSTOMER WHO LOOKS LIKE A WALKING SPORTS-LOGO BILLBOARD (ALTHOUGH YOU ARE NOT SURE WHAT THE SPORTS ARE, EXACTLY — MOUNTAIN BIKING AND SNOWBOARDING, MAYBE?) AND TRY TO BE GLAD THAT HE IS AT LEAST TALKING TO YOU LIKE A HUMAN BEING AND NOT A ROBOT ONLY HERE TO SERVE HIM.

YOU STEER HIM TO THE . . .

POETRY SECTION.

POETRY?

HIM? IT'S WHAT HE ASKED FOR.

GOTTA SHELVE BOOKS.

12:30

SHELVED. BOXED RETURNS. LABELED BOXES.

WHEW.

Poetry guy STILL there.

Two books under his arm.

Head buried in a third.

You head in his direction to see who his poets of choice are.

It's a mix. Whitman. Adrienne Rich. And Baudelaire.

Maybe I'll have to check them out sometime.

MUCH LATER (As In, If Your Parents Were Around, They'd Be Saying Subtle Parent Things Like "It's Getting Late")

Mr. W snags you as you are pondering the poets.

"It's slow for the moment," he says. "Why don't you take lunch now, Christopher?"

"Okay," you say.

You will check receipts later to see what poetry books went out in your absence.

You are headed out the door when you meet...

Brendan.

"I'll sell you a book," you tell him. "But then I've got my lunch break."

"Come to the diner with me," Brendan suggests.

You agree.

You are, you confess now, strangely nervous.

WHAT are you going to talk to Brendan about?

You've never hung around with him alone before.

You hang around with, let's face it, girls.

The guys who are your friends? Two. Whom you've known forever. Jason, with whom you no longer have a thing in common. And Alex...away.

Being treated. For depression. And a suicide attempt.

These are your guy friends.

Sometimes you miss Jason.

You definitely miss Alex. But you've barely kept in touch with him and he's not big on keeping in touch with you either.

You want him back. Better.

But meanwhile, girls are easier to be friends with.

Girls talk about things besides sports and (duh) babes.

You review your sports data.

You realize you pretty much used it up the night before.

What would John Wayne do???

Phone.

12:15 A.M.

PARENTS. THEY ACTUALLY SAY WHEN YOU TELL THEM WHAT TIME IT IS HERE: "IT'S GETTING LATE, ISN'T IT?"

YOU SAY, "IT'S SATURDAY NIGHT."

YOUR MOTHER SAYS, "OH? DID YOU HAVE A DATE?"

"NO," YOU SAY.

THE CONVERSATION PRETTY MUCH LOSES IT FROM THERE.

BUT YOU WERE WRITING ABOUT THE BOOKSTORE.

ACTUALLY, CUT TO THE DINER. YOU AND BRENDAN HAVE DONE SOME SPORTS TALK ON THE WAY THERE.

AFTER YOU'VE ORDERED, YOU REACH DEEP AND SAY, "WHO DO YOU LIKE IN THE WNBA?"

BRENDAN GIVES YOU A STRANGE LOOK. "PHOENIX STILL RULES FOR ME," HE SAYS.

THEN HE SAYS, "BUT I'M NOT THAT BIG ON SPORTS."

"ME NEITHER," YOU SAY, WAY TOO QUICKLY.

TO COVER YOUR MAJOR SPORTS KNOWLEDGE GAP, YOU TELL BRENDAN ABOUT THE POET/LOGO JOCK AND HE LAUGHS.

AFTER THAT, YOU ARE NOT SO WORRIED ABOUT TALKING TO HIM. TRUE, IT'S NOT LIKE HANGING OUT WITH ALEX. WITH ALEX YOU COULD GO OFF ABOUT YOUR FANTASY OF BECOMING A COWBOY OR DISCUSS THE LATEST BABY-SITTER/HOUSEKEEPER YOUR PARENTS HAD LEFT BEHIND TO LOOK AFTER YOU WHILE THEY DID THEIR VANISHING ACT.

But you had history with Alex and besides, you were younger then.

You no longer fantasize about becoming a cowboy.

And your parents no longer leave you with a baby-sitter/housekeeper.

Brendan actually asks you what it's like not to have your parents around. You say living on takeout is not as much fun when it's a 24/7 option.

Then, so you don't sound as if you're feeling sorry for yourself, you say that the freedom is great.

Brendan nods.

He doesn't talk about his parents, so you don't ask. (Can't tell a book by its cover.)

You find yourself telling him a little about Alex. (Not a lot about Alex, though. Maybe the whole school talks about what happened, you don't know, but he's got a right to his privacy and you're not going to talk about it. Besides, it's hard to talk about even to your closest friends.)

So you chat and chew and Brendan tells you a little about his old school.

You ask, before you think, if his old school had Cro Mags in it and he looks puzzled.

So then you have to explain that Cro Mags is short for Cro-Magnon cavepeople.

"The jocks at school? Those are universal," he says.

"I'm not sure if that is good news or bad news," you say, and he laughs.

Ducky the entertainer.

Somehow, the conversation shifts around to the girls at school.

"You know a lot of them," he says.

Bond. James Bond. A girl in every locker.

"Friends," you say. "Somehow, this past year, we started hanging out and became friends. You're not sure how to explain it, other than that.

Luckily, Brendan doesn't ask deep questions. He nods and says, "Well, about Amalia. Is it my imagination, or has she been a little distant lately?"

"Amalia," you say. "Distant?"

He nods. "Ever since I came back from camp. She's nice. She's friendly. She laughs at my jokes and we go out. But she's — I don't know. It's like she's taken a step back."

"Oh." You decide it's better not to mention you noticed it too.

"I don't think there's anybody else," Brendan says.

He pauses.

Your cue.

"No," you agree. You tell him you're sure about that.

He looks relieved for a moment.

"She's not like that," you add.

"I didn't think so," Brendan says. "But for some reason I don't feel as if I know her the way I did at the beginning of the summer."

You're not sure what the problem is either. "Give it time," you say.

Lame, but serviceable.

Brendan nods. "It's what I figured," he says. Then he switches to you, as in:

B: What about you and Sunny?

D: ????

B: You know, like dating?

D: [Nervous laughter.]

B: Seriously.

So you tell him you'd never be interested in Sunny that way. And you know she wouldn't be interested in you that way either.

Brendan says, "Don't kid yourself. I've seen the way she looks at you."

Those looks! Is that what they mean?

You want to slide down under the table and stay there.

You reject the whole idea. What does Brendan know?

You laugh again and say, "Why ruin a beautiful friendship?"

Then you say, "I'd better get back to work."

You talk with Brendan about working in the bookstore on the way back. Your dramatic account of the shoplifter lasts most of the trip. Then you say good-bye to Brendan...although you can't say good-bye to what Brendan said.

How could Brendan be so off base about you and Sunny?

Can't a guy and a girl be friends without the whole world making something of it? Why is that so hard for the world to accept?

And Sunny would never go for it, anyway.

Even if it was a possibility.

Which it is NOT.

Aug. 22

Sunday.
Not. Possible.

No reason to go there.
You're Ducky.
She's Sunny.
You're friends.
End of story.

Aug. 23
2:23 P.M.

Mondays at the bookstore are S...L...O...W....
Not that bookstores are usually party scenes.
Mr. W came in and opened the store with Sunny.
When you get here at 2:00 he bolts.

Leaving you and Sunny alone together.

Stop this.

You and Sunny and ninety gazillion books and a
whole store full of people.

For a moment you are tempted to think about
asking Jay (the friend formerly known as Jason) for his
advice.

He dates girls. He listens to the Cro Mags talk about dating girls.

The girls who go out with those guys seem ordinary and nice.

(THEN WHY ARE THEY DATING CRO MAGS????)

Maybe Jay could give you some help.

Then you remember his stupid efforts to introduce you to girls. Any girls. As if girls were interchangeable. As if people were interchangeable.

You do not need Jay's advice.

Besides, this isn't a girl-guy thing. Just because Brendan said so, that doesn't make it true.

He's way off base. Out of the ballpark. In another game.

Jay would just start talking about what a "babe" Sunny is.

She is cute.

Well, pretty.

Beautiful, maybe.

Here she comes.

Stash this.

You have shelved books. Tallied receipts. Boxed returns. Unpacked books.

You are NOT going to vacuum. No housework at the bookstore.

Sunny has spent some quality time in the coffee room. The boxes of tea are in alphabetical order. The sink sparkles. She's put hooks under the cabinet to hang the mugs on, so they're not jammed on the table with the coffeepot and microwave.

It now looks neat, clean, organized.

She brings you a cup of hot tea.

You discuss the coffee that the bookstore keeps on hand for Mr W and employees.

Sunny says she has a plan. She is going to start using the petty cash and buying decent coffee when her father isn't around. She'll put it in the old coffee tins and maybe he'll never notice that he never has to buy a new can of coffee.

It's a plan, you concede.

"Meanwhile, I made you tea because the coffee is vile," Sunny says.

"Tarbucks," you offer and Sunny laughs. You notice that her eyes crinkle in a good way when she does.

WELL, YOU'D NOTICED IT BEFORE. NOW YOU NOTICE IT
AGAIN.

STOP. THIS.

AUG. 24
9:45 P.M.
AVOIDING THE SUBJECT

"HI," SUNNY SAYS. "IT'S ME."

"HI," YOU SAY.

THEN YOU RUN OUT OF THINGS TO SAY.

SUNNY DOESN'T NOTICE.

DOES SHE?

SHE TELLS YOU MAGGIE IS HANGING IN THERE. SHE
REPORTS THAT DAWN WANTS TO "EXPLORE MORE PIERCINGS"
BUT THAT HER FATHER HAS SAID A BIG NO. SHE SAYS SHE
DREAMS OF OWNING A RETRO BOWLING SHIRT WITH HER NAME
EMBROIDERED ON THE POCKET. SHE WANTS TO FIND IT JUST
HANGING ON THE RACK. OR BETTER YET, IN A BIG BIN OF
JUMBLED-UP CLOTHES, THE KIND THAT VINTAGE STORES PUT
OUT FOR BUCK-A-BAG SALES.

"IT WOULD BOWL YOU OVER?" YOU OFFER.

SUNNY LAUGHS. HARD.

ARE YOUR JOKES THAT FUNNY?

Or is this some girl-guy thing?

You are not ready for this. This is not for publication, but you aren't ready.

At least, you're pretty sure you aren't.

You are not going to write about it anymore. You're going to write about something else.

9:55 P.M.

Okay. You're home now. You can stop thinking about the Sunny situation.

10:03

Anything else.

10:30

That's it. You're down for the night.

10:33

Well, at least you didn't write about that subject again.

Aug. 25
Late A.M. Wednesday.

Park. Bike. You.

Thinking.

Are you laughing too hard at Sunny's jokes?

Being around her makes you feel like laughing, generally. You feel, you know, pretty good.

Oxygenated.

Caffeinated.

But in a good way.

You've always laughed at her jokes. She's always laughed at yours. You get each other's sense of humor.

If you stop laughing at Sunny's jokes now, it's going to be bizarre.

Break room. Bookstore.

Did Sunny just ask you on a date? Is "Hey, wanna catch the extremely bad action flick at the plex when we're out of here?" a date invitation?

Evidence:

For:

You suggest calling up the rest of the gang, to maximize the sounds of disgust, throwing popcorn-at-the-screen potential.

Sunny says, "Nah, let's just go together."

You say, "Sure."

Then you bolt in here and grab the old journal like a life raft.

Against:

It's Sunny. And you. FRIENDS.

This is all Brendan's fault.

Yeah. Brendan. You'll blame him.

Like that's going to fix things now.

Besides, it's not Brendan's fault.

Stop freaking, Ducky. Just act like yourself.

This is not a situation, except in your own DUCK BRAIN.

6:10 P.M.

Mr. W is having an in-depth discussion with a new potential full-timer.

She looks okay.

With school starting soon, he's going to need someone full-time.

But that's not what is important here. You are avoiding the subject.

You are propped near the bookstore entrance, scribbling.

While Sunny is CHANGING.

As in, slipping into the bathroom to change clothes from her work clothes to something else for going to the movies.

You think about this WAY too much. Like, did she bring clothes from home just for this NOT DATE?

Is she getting dressed up?

Did she plan the whole thing?

Should you — what?

BREATH MINTS.

Gotta go.

LATER. EONS LATER. MIND-ALTERING, TIME-TRAVELING,
SIGNIFICANT AMOUNTS OF TIME LATER.

REALLY ONLY 11:20 ON AN ORDINARY WEDNESDAY NIGHT.
YOU WISH.

OKAY. BACK TO PRE "IT'S NOT A DATE" PANIC.

YOU BUY TWO PACKS OF BREATH MINTS AT THE
PHARMACY AND EAT ABOUT SIX ON THE WAY BACK TO THE
BOOKSTORE.

YOUR WHOLE BRAIN SMELLS LIKE PEPPERMINT.

FORTUNATELY, SUNNY DOESN'T NOTICE WHEN SHE
EMERGES FROM THE BREAK ROOM.

SHE LOOKS GOOD. THE FLITTY TOP THING ESPECIALLY.
DEFINITELY DRESSIER THAN BOOKSTORE MODE.

"NICE LOOK," YOU SAY.

SUNNY SMILES AND HER EYES CRINKLE AND YOU BLURT
OUT, "WANT TO GET SOMETHING TO EAT?"

"GREAT IDEA," SHE SAYS, AND HER EYES CRINKLE EVEN
MORE.

YOU PRACTICALLY RUN FROM THE BOOKSTORE. YOU DO
NOT REMEMBER SUNNY SAYING GOOD-BYE TO HER FATHER
AND TELLING HIM YOU'LL BRING HER HOME LATER (ALTHOUGH
YOU KNOW SHE MUST HAVE).

YOU DO NOT REMEMBER HOW YOU ENDED UP IN GALAXY
DELUXE.

But there you are in the brand-new retro joint, staring at the menu while Sunny admires the bowling-trophy decor.

You do not remember what you ate.

You do remember part of the movie. It's so bad that you and Sunny are collapsing against each other laughing.

You are whispering the action hero's lines before he says them.

The girl — the damsel in distress — stands around looking slightly malnourished and screaming a lot.

Just like in the John Wayne movies of ancient history, except those girls looked better fed.

Don't the people who make movies get it?

Clearly not. And you yourself DID just pay money to see this old-fashioned, high-tech piece of junk.

And then, Sunny takes your hand while she is in a mid-laughing fit.

She's grabbed your hand before.

But this feels different.

Plus, she doesn't let go.

That's the last thing about the movie you remember.

You regain consciousness as your car pulls up outside Sunny's house.

She is shaking her head. "Too much, Ducky," she says.

Too much what? What have you been talking about?

You must have been acting normal because she is not giving you Planet Ducky looks.

"It's been fun," you say, to conceal the fact that you are recovering from some kind of amnesia attack.

You have your hand back. Soon, surely, your mind will follow.

Sunny puts her hand on the door. In the dark, you see the flash of her teeth as she smiles at you.

Then, without warning, she leans forward and...

KISSES you.

On the mouth.

And it's not a just-friends kiss either.

You freeze. Your lips freeze.

The night freezes.

You do not, however, lose consciousness as you did in the movie.

On the contrary, you are much TOO CONSCIOUS.

Sunny does not appear to have noticed the lip chill or the parallel icing over of the local universe.

She pulls back, smiles again, and says softly, "'Night, Ducky."

She slides out of the car and is gone.

Sunny kissed you, Ducky. On the mouth. With, well, feeling.

Brendan was right.

You were wrong.

You sit in the car until you realize that Sunny might think you are sitting there thinking about the kiss.

Which you are, but not in THAT way.

You are thinking in a panicked, where's-the-rabbit-hole kind of way.

You start the car and drive, careful not to burn rubber or show any other signs of fear or derangement.

You feel . . . MISERABLE.

Is this the end of a beautiful friendship?

Then you think, What is wrong with you?

You just got kissed.

What is the problem here?

Midnight
When a Kiss Is Not Just a Kiss

You don't care if you do have work tomorrow. You realize that you need to stay up and worry about this.

Sunny kissed you. You did not kiss her back. Your heart raced, but not with passion. It was another P word.

Panic.

It felt...not right. As if it were happening to someone else. Like an experiment that failed.

What does that mean?

Of all the girls in all the world, Sunny would be the one you'd choose. But you're not at all happy she chose you.

You don't want to be chosen. Not like that. Not by Sunny.

WHAT IS WRONG WITH YOU???

Sunny is perfect for you. You are perfect for her.

Except for that kiss thing. That lack of he-she chemistry.

It's like you need a new chemistry set....

Enough with the similes. Or maybe I mean metaphors.

Whatever.

I am not going to think about this anymore.

I'll deal with it tomorrow.

And hey, maybe you were wrong. You read way too much into it. It was just a

Kiss.

Post work.

Post ruining Sunny's life, possibly.

Okay, maybe you didn't ruin her life, but when she bounded into work smiling and saying, "Ducky!" like she hadn't seen you forever and looked like she'd like to throw her arms around you if she could, you didn't have to look the way you did.

What way?

With a frozen face. Like a duck in headlights.

Sunny's megawatt smile dims.

You say, "Uh, hi, Sunny."

She's still smiling on her way to the break room, but it's more like one of those customer-friendly models.

You fling yourself at an unsuspecting customer, who is a little taken aback at the detail with which you explain the Frequent Customer discount policy.

She finally cuts you off with a "Just looking, thanks."

You straighten a few books on the long, long, LONG walk back to the register where Sunny is sitting, holding a mug of coffee.

"You made the coffee switch?" you begin to babble.

"Cool. I think I'll get me some. Has your father noticed? Well, I guess not if you just did it, huh?"

"Ducky," she says.

You stop babbling.

She says, "Hey, Ducky. Relax. It was just a kiss. You were in the right place at the right time, that's all."

"Yeah?" you say, trying to keep your tone neutral.

You cannot fool Sunny.

She knows you.

But you don't know her at all. What does the look she is giving you now mean?

"Hey, nothing personal, okay?" she says.

She pats your arm and winks at you.

You feel scalded.

Sunny says, "I did sneak in some new coffee. Just made it. I'll go get you a cup."

You watch Sunny walk away and you hope she is still your friend.

You take the coffee when she returns. You say, "You know, Sunny, you are one of the most important people in my life."

Sunny laughs and it sort of scares you. But she says, "Silly boy, I better be. Now stop brooding. Or I'm not going to ask you out to play with me again."

How could she be so...sophisticated?

"I don't want to mess us up," you blunder on.

"Keep talking like that, you will," she shoots back. Light. Fast. A smile with glitter on it.

You get the hint. Sunny is smiling but that is not a happy smile.

It's a smile that says: <u>Shut up, Ducky. You've hurt my feelings.</u>

So you shut up.

And you stay that way the rest of the day.

You do not laugh, together or separately. Not once.

Not even when Mr W stares down at his mug of coffee and goes, "Good coffee. I guess I ought to wash out my cup more often."

8:15 P.M.
Later Thursday

You cannot call the people you would normally call. Dawn, Maggie, and Amalia are all too close to Sunny.

You will not call Jay.

Telling Jay would be like telling the world.

Besides, he would laugh at you.

He might also suspect that this is your first real kiss.

And if he asks you, you will not be able to lie.

Furthermore, he will start calling you all those stupid nicknames he's made out of Ducky. Duckman, Duckorama, Duckster.

You do not need that.

And yet . . . and yet . . .

Somewhat Later

Saved by the Ted.

Just as you are reaching for the phone you hear: the back door, then the refrigerator door, then a cabinet door.

Ted is home.

You decide you will talk to Ted.

You find him in the kitchen, shoving cereal into his mouth like there's a shortage.

"Hey, Ted," you say.

"Ucky," he mumbles around the mouthful of cereal.

"Can I talk to you?"

He swallows the cereal. "I'll clean the kitchen. I know it's my turn. I will."

Is that how Ted sees you? The person who nags about housecleaning?

"Okay," you say. "Listen, could I talk to you about something else?"

So he listens to you while you listen to him slurp up the rest of the cereal as you tell him the whole pathetic story. Except that you don't mention the kiss was Numero Uno.

He looks at you when you finish and says, "You don't like her?"

"Yes I like her," you say. "But not like that. I mean, you know, kissing her didn't do it for me. It was like, well, I don't know...."

"Sometimes it works and sometimes it doesn't," says Ted, Big Man on Campus.

"Yeah, well, what do you do when it doesn't?"

Ted shrugs. He says, "Ducky. She'll get over it. You'll get over it. And hey. Maybe you just need more practice together."

He makes a kissy noise.

Cro Mag.

You leave. "Don't forget to clean the kitchen" is your lame parting shot.

"You're welcome," he shouts after you.

Ted is useless. USELESS. Why expect him to be understanding and sensitive when he can be an OBNOXIOUS BIG BROTHER?

Do they have schools for this? How do people learn to be so completely OBNOXIOUS? Are they born this way?

Jay wasn't. Back when he was Jason, before he started hanging with the Cro Mags, he was normal. Okay.

Ted, you think you remember, had moments when he wasn't a snotty older brother, when you were younger. He'd take you along sometimes and not complain too much.

He was protective of you when the other kids circled like sharks.

But now he's the brother from the planet Lug.

10:01

So you've called Brendan.

You hope it's not too weird, but you are desperate.

He is, after all, the one who brought this up in

THE FIRST PLACE. YOU HAVE DECIDED HE IS NOT TO BLAME,
BUT YOU ARE STILL INCLUDING HIM IN THIS WHOLE MESS.

Amazingly, Brendan is at home. You thought he
had a date with Amalia.

"What happened to your date?" you blurt out.

Tactful, Ducky.

She canceled, he tells you. "It's Maggie. She
showed up at Amalia's and she was, according to
Amalia, pretty upset."

You don't ask if it is about Maggie's mom.

It is always about Maggie's mom.

"Poor Maggie," you say.

"Yeah." He changes the subject. "What's up?"

"Advice," you say. "About Sunny."

"Yeah?" He sounds expectant.

"We had a date," you begin.

"What did I tell you! She likes you."

"Wait," you say. You tell him the whole story, more
or less.

The less being that you don't get too specific
about the kiss. As in, she seemed to enjoy it, but you
did not.

You conclude by saying, "So maybe you were right,
Brendan. Maybe Sunny does sort of like me."

"But?" he says. "I hear doubts."

"I like Sunny too," you say. "I love Sunny. But not like that."

Not in THAT WAY.

Split screen, Brendan flipping through the TV channels while he talks, you clutching the phone, bug-eyed with panic.

B: Whoa.

D: Keanu Reeves says that in every movie, did you know that?

B: Really. Well.

[Silence]

B: Okay. Well. This could be a problem. I don't mind telling you, just between us, that Amalia mentioned what a great couple she thought you and Sunny would make.

D: She did? Great.

B: Yeah.

D: What am I going to do?

B. I don't know. What do you want to do?

D: I don't know. I guess I just want things to be the way they were.

B: That is not going to be easy. It may not be possible.

D: But I ... Sunny ... We ...

B: You've gotta do something fast, you know. The

longer you let it go, the worse it's going to get. It's too bad.

D: What is?

B: That you and Sunny are such good friends. If it was just, you know, a normal date that didn't work, you could smile at each other in the halls and let it go.

D: Great. Just great.

B: Unless you're mistaken?

D: No.

B: Well then, you can't be attracted to her if you're not. You shouldn't try to talk yourself into it. That's not fair to her or you. You'll just end up hurting her worse if you try to fake it. So go with the truth. That's how to do it.

D: It's brutal.

B: Not so bad. The alternative is worse.

D: [gulp] Okay. Right. Thanks.

B: Anytime.

Cut to Ducky, sprawled on the floor of his room, wishing he were somebody else. A Cro Mag, for example. A being without feelings. Or at least, the appearance of feelings.

What if I'm just a coward? What if I have—commitment issues?

What if I'm afraid to get involved?

Sunny would be the perfect girlfriend. We'd make a great couple. We like the same things. We share the same fashion sense. We're so close anyway.

Why not get closer?

Why not?

Why not?

Why don't I feel it?

Aug. 27
Friday
Lunch Break at Work

Sunny called in sick. This is a BAD SIGN.

Mr. W says she's fine when you ask.

You have a paranoid moment wondering whether he's thinking, HE HURT MY LITTLE GIRL, THE CREEP.

But you know Sunny hasn't said anything to him.

"I hope she feels better," you say.

You HAVE hurt her. You ARE a creep. An insensitive CRD MAG.

You reshelve books. You brood.

Wait a minute.

You didn't kiss Sunny.

She kissed you.

You didn't even kiss back. She just didn't notice.

There's Dawn.

Gotta go.

Afternoon Break. On a Bench, Outside

Dawn actually found a couple of books for a customer and ended up helping you shelve for awhile.

She kept the conversation light.

She did not talk about Sunny.

You did not talk about Sunny.

This lack of the mention of Sunny's name leads you to believe that Sunny has talked about you to Dawn.

But you can't ask her, since she is more Sunny's friend than yours.

Terrific. Are you now going to have to divide your friends into "Sunny's" and "Ducky's"?

Like you have friends to spare.

What are you going to do?

BENCH-RIDING OUTSIDE THE BOOKSTORE. AGAIN.

DON'T FEEL LIKE GOING HOME.

AMALIA JUST LEFT.

SHE SAID, "DUCKY, I NEED TO TALK TO YOU."

JOHN WAYNE NEVER RAN FROM A FIGHT, BUT YOU'RE
PRETTY SURE THOSE WORDS WOULD HAVE MADE HIM THINK
TWICE.

SO SHE CAN TALK TO YOU, YOU JUST CAN'T TALK TO HER.
THIS IS MEAN AND PETTY AND LOW AND IT'S HOW YOU FEEL.
THE BASIC FACTS.

BUT YOU ARE DUCKY THE UNDERSTANDING, FRIEND TO
ALL, BOYFRIEND TO NONE.

YOU NOD. YOU SAY OKAY. YOU'RE JUST FINISHING FOR THE
DAY.

YOU GO TO THE LOCAL BEAN 'N' BREW, GET
CAPPUCCINOS, AND STAKE OUT THE BENCH.

YOU SAY, "SO, WHAT'S UP?"

TO YOUR ENORMOUS, COWARDLY, WHAT-A-ROTTEN-
FRIEND-YOU-ARE RELIEF, AMALIA SAYS, "IT'S MAGGIE."

"MAGGIE," YOU SAY, AND LET OUT A SAVED, WHEW,
SIGH.

BECAUSE YOU ("HI, I'M DUCKY, THE CENTER OF THE
KNOWN UNIVERSE. EVERYTHING IS ABOUT ME") WERE

actually afraid she had come to talk to you about Sunny. And you.

Amalia nods. She thinks you're sighing in sympathy.

"Yeah," she says.

Then she tells you about the hours Maggie spent at her house the night before, all torn up about her mother.

She tells you that Maggie can't take much more of this.

She tells you that something's got to give.

"Maggie has to confront her home life or she's gonna blow," Amalia says. "Explode. Break down. Something. I don't know what."

"As long as you're there for her, maybe she won't," you say.

Then you feel like a complete jerk.

You tried to be there for Alex, and did it help? No. You couldn't save him. Couldn't help him.

The best you could do was send him to the ER.

And now you barely hear from him at the treatment center.

Being there for someone is, in your opinion, not always the best advice.

But what other advice can you offer?

Amalia sighs. Big. "Yeah," she says, her voice as unconvincing as your lame offer of sympathy.

"You could...well, maybe you could talk to Mrs. Blume with Maggie. You know, be there for moral support."

"Somehow, I don't think Maggie would go for that."

She's right.

So you decide to do the original, the obvious. You decide to change the subject. "Talked to Brendan last night," you say. "He's decent, you know?"

"Yeah," says Amalia, her tone even less convincing. Distinctly lacking in enthusiasm.

"Yeah?" you say. "That's it?"

Relief at not being grilled about Sunny makes you bold. Giddy. Reckless.

You say, "What's going on, Amalia? With you and Brendan?"

Your tone is no-nonsense. Authoritative.

Very John Wayne.

Amalia succumbs to your tough-guy act.

She says, "Brendan is great."

"But?" you prompt.

"But...he's too great, you know? I mean, maybe he's too good for me. It's scary how nice he is, how...I mean, what if it doesn't last? It'll hurt. Big time. Why suffer if you don't have to?"

"Because you like Brendan?"

"Yeah." Like this is bad news.

You want to tell her the bad news is when you don't like someone. Someone you count on. Someone who is like family to you.

Big Amalia sigh. She adds, "I'm just going to try to keep it light."

You say, "C'mon, Amalia. Why be afraid of admitting you care about Brendan?"

"I'm not afraid! It's not that. Really," she says. "It's just...self-respect. Common sense. Reason."

"Nope. Fear," you say. Fearlessly.

She shakes her head, looks down. Doesn't answer.

"Don't be afraid. If it's right...you can't be afraid."

(It's when it is wrong that you should be afraid.)

She jumps up. "Gotta go. Later," she says, and hurries away without meeting your eyes.

Was she crying?

Good work, Ducky.

But you know you're right.

Ask the love doctor. He'll tell you the truth.

Except about himself.

WAY PAST MIDNIGHT

The phone rings at 5 of midnight. This hour, you figure it's the parents, still wrestling with that old time-zone problem of theirs.

Another few years, they may get it.

You also figure that your brother will sleep through the ringing. So you grab the phone and croak, "Hello?"

"Ducky," a strangled voice says.

"It's me," you say, still half asleep and not quite sure of who is calling you.

"It's Maggie," says the voice. Little. Scared. Tear-filled.

Not like Maggie's voice at all.

"Maggie," you say. "What's wrong?" You are awake now. And a little freaked.

And guess what? You do not think this is about you.

"Can you pick me up at my house? Like, right now?" she says in a low, hoarse whisper.

"Now," you repeat. You realize you do that a lot these days — repeat words to stall for time.

BUT WHY DO YOU NEED TO STALL FOR TIME? THERE IS
ONLY ONE RIGHT ANSWER.

"PLEASE," SHE WHISPERS URGENTLY.

"I'M ON MY WAY," YOU SAY AT THE SAME MOMENT.

"OH, DUCKY," SHE SAYS AND HANGS UP THE PHONE.

YOUR BRO IS STILL SLEEPING LIKE A BABY WHEN YOU
ROCKET OFF THE PREMISES.

YOU LEAVE HIM A NOTE.

LIKE HE'S EVER GONNA WAKE UP AND NOTICE YOUR
ABSENCE.

YOU GET TO THE BLUMES' AND THINK MAYBE YOU
SHOULDN'T RING THE DOORBELL, SINCE IT IS SO LATE.

THEN YOU NOTICE THAT LIGHTS ARE ON. EVERYWHERE. IF
THE HOUSE WERE ANY BRIGHTER, IT WOULD LOOK AS IF IT
WERE ON FIRE.

AND IT WOULD BE A BIG FIRE TOO, CONSIDERING THE SIZE
OF THE HOUSE.

YOU RING THE BELL.

THE DOOR OPENS A CRACK. YOU SEE ONE OF MAGGIE'S
EYES. SHE WHISPERS, "WE'LL BE RIGHT OUT."

YOU CAN BARELY HEAR HER. NOT BECAUSE SHE IS
WHISPERING.

BECAUSE SOMEONE IS SHOUTING IN THERE.

LOUD, INCOHERENT SHOUTING. YOU HEAR THINGS
BREAKING. YOU HEAR MUSIC TURNED WAY UP.

You flinch at the sound of something big smashed into small pieces as Maggie shuts the door in your face.

Moments later Maggie emerges—holding Zeke's hand. He's still pj'd but he's wide-awake. His eyes have that round, little-kid look. Scared, sleepy, like maybe it's all just a nightmare that Mommy will come fix.

Mommy's not available, kid. She might as well be in Crete.

You're pretty sure about that, even though Maggie says not one word to you on the ride back to your house. She just rocks Zeke and makes this crooning sound.

You lead the way into the house, not sure what else to do.

You stash Maggie and Zeke in the parents' room, which has its own bathroom, in case Zeke has any off-hour runs to make.

You haul out clean sheets and produce clean towels.

"We'll take care of it," Maggie says. She hands the towels to Zeke. "Why don't you go put these in the bathroom for us," she says.

He obeys. He seems glad to have a job to do.

You say to Maggie, as she stands in the door of the room, "Are you okay?" figuring maybe she sent Zeke away so you could have a quick chat.

"Yes," she says. "Thank you, Ducky. Thank you for not asking any questions."

"No problem," you say, taking the hint. "Good night. Call me if you need anything."

Maggie nods. It is the nod of a tired, much older woman.

She closes the door.

You feel like you should stay awake and keep watch. Sit outside the door.

Pace the hall.

But you know this is pointless.

Time to zzz.

Like Ted's been doing this whole time.

Aug. 28
Saturday
8:45 A.M.

You wake up. You think you've gone to sleep with the radio on.

Because you are hearing voices.

But no. The little voices are NOT coming from the bedside box.

They're coming from ... the kitchen.

You throw on some clothes, speed to the kitchen, and hover outside the kitchen door.

The voices are Maggie's and Ted's. They are chatting away like old friends.

Time to make a guest appearance before Ted says something really stupid.

10:30 A.M., More or Less

Ted is a jerk.

As you walk into the kitchen and say good morning, he gives you this BIG, TOTALLY OBNOXIOUS guy-to-guy wink.

His eyes cut to Maggie.

You get it.

You wish you didn't.

Ted the Dumb thinks Maggie is your girlfriend and that she has spent the night.

Maggie doesn't catch this, of course. She is pouring you a cup of coffee.

You give Ted your death-ray look.

Then all is redeemed by Zeke trekking down the hall calling, "Maggie? Maggie, I'm hungry!"

Ted is blown away. The random collection of cells he calls a brain crashes.

As Zeke comes into the kitchen, you enjoy the moment.

In Ted's limited universe, Zeke does not compute.

I give Ted a big, BIG wink. "Later," I say.

Ted recovers (give him credit for SOMETHING) and makes conversation with Zeke.

"When did you get here?" Ted asks.

"Late," says Zeke. "Can I have any cereal I want?"

"One bowl," says Maggie firmly. "But you can put any cereal you want into it."

"Right," says Ted. "Be my guest." He jumps up and begins lining up cereal boxes on the table.

When he is finished he looks from you to Maggie to Zeke. He shakes his head.

"Gotta go," he says. "Nice to see you, Maggie, Zeke."

"Bye," Zeke says.

Maggie gulps down some OJ. You go into your breakfast-chef routine and manage to put together pancakes. Zeke demands three, and Maggie accepts the two you offer. You compromise on the missing-syrup issue by heating apple jelly in the microwave. You tell Zeke it is special apple syrup.

He goes for it. He's a good kid.

Maggie forks up the pancakes and tells you, politely, that they're good. She drinks MORE juice.

Silence.

You get that Maggie doesn't want to talk about it. You don't ask questions.

You can wait her out.

It's Zeke who says, "I like this better than my house. I hate my house. Why can't Dad come home? Why can't he make Mom act right?"

That about covers it, you figure.

You and Zeke both look at Maggie.

Zeke says, "Don't we count as much as his movie?"

Maggie speaks at last. "Good point, Zeke," she says slowly. "We should count at least that much. We should."

"Yeah," says Zeke. He eats more pancakes.

"He's right," you say. "Your father should be here. This is too much for you, Maggie. Way too much. It's not fair — to Zeke or you. Or to your mother, if you want to go there."

"I don't," Maggie answers. She stands up, takes dishes to the sink, rinses them, and loads them in the petrified forest of dirty dishes in the dishwasher.

She takes a box of dishwasher soap off the counter and sets the dishwasher to work.

"Maggie?" you say.

She answers, "May I use your phone?"

You nod at the phone on the kitchen counter. She grabs it and dials. "Dad?" she says. "It's me. You have to come home. Now. Things are out of control.... No. Now.... I mean it, Dad.... No, you can't call me back later. Zeke and I aren't home. We couldn't... Mom was out of control."

She pauses to listen for a minute.

"No," she says.

She listens some more.

"NO!" she says. "You come home now or I'm going to turn Mom in to the police. I mean it."

Zeke's eyes go round.

She listens. She says, "All right, then."

She hangs up.

She looks sooo relieved.

"He's catching the next plane back," she says.

Zeke says, "The police?"

"No way, Zeke. Don't worry. I was just being tough with Dad."

"Oh," he says.

I meet Maggie's eyes. "Good for you," I say.

Bookstore. Afternoon Break. Baby-sitting

You are baby-sitting in the bookstore. That means that Zeke is reading in the kids' section. You are sitting in the beanbag chair (kid-sized, but adequate), making sure he stays safe and happy, more or less.

He's taking all this in stride. After his astute situational commentary this A.M., he's kept to himself.

You hadn't intended to bring Maggie and Zeke to work, but what else could you do with them? Leaving them alone in your house isn't a kind thing.

You've learned to live in the cave. You've learned that if you keep your room clean, the chaos and grime do not bother you. Too much.

But Maggie is different.

Sunny and Maggie are hauling out boxes of display props. Mr. W. has been looking sad — missing Mrs. W, I think. He touches some of the items in the boxes and then backs away.

Sunny catches him at it.

She says, "Dad. Mom's watching you shirk your work."

For a moment, Mr. W is still. Then he smiles. Not a 100% smile, but a smile. His eyes meet Sunny's and she gives him the same kind of smile back.

They seem closer than they've ever been. Tighter. A real family unit of two.

You remember then that Sunny told you that her mother was very into organizing special seasonal windows. She collected props from everywhere: yard sales, catalogs, crafts supply houses. She also made them.

This explains the Barbies on the beach. It's not just a Sunny thing.

It's a Sunny-and-her-mom thing.

"Look at this," Sunny says. "I made this. Well, Mom and I did." She holds up a small papier-mâché tree. "We used a paper-towel roll to build the trunk. The branches are made of chopsticks saved from the Thai takeout...."

"Cool," says Maggie. "Maybe Zeke and I can make something for the window collection."

"Good idea," Mr. W says.

Sunny has barely spoken to you. She's not ignoring you in a mean way.

She's just not quite looking at you. Shying away from you.

You. Feel. Rotten.

You'd feel worse, but you are exhausted from the night before. You didn't stay up guarding Maggie and Zeke (from what?) but you didn't sleep all that well either.

Mr. W is doing something on the computer.

You watch Zeke and listen as Maggie says in a low voice, "I know Mom can't help it. I know that, Sunny. But it doesn't help anymore. I mean, when I was out of control about my eating, I kept thinking I was in control, you know? And I bet Mom feels the same way. But it's no good. She's got to stop. For me. For Zeke. For Dad. For herself."

"You're right," Sunny says softly.

And then you hear Maggie start to cry.

Zeke has put down his book. He is now in puzzle heaven. He doesn't notice.

Sunny and Maggie go to the back of the store and stay there for a long time. When they come out of the break room, Maggie's eyes are a little red. She looks tired.

But she is still standing.

4:28 P.M.

Less rotten. More confused.

Sunny just came up to you and whispered, "Maggie's told me everything. What you did last night was a good thing, Ducky."

"Uh," you say.

But Sunny has already walked away.

6:02

Arrivals and departures.

Mr. Blume just showed up to scoop up Maggie and Zeke.

I think Maggie wanted to cry. But she wouldn't let herself. She folded her arms and glared at her father.

I think she has a right to be angry with him.

Zeke flung himself at his father. Mr. Blume looked...shocked?

Mr. Blume thanked me. He thanked Sunny.

Maggie kept her arms folded. Only as they were leaving did she unfold them.

Zeke took one of his father's hands.

Maggie took Zeke's other hand.

What are they going to find at home?

WHAT? WHAT?

She gave you this blank, cold, unfriendly look.

You thought it meant for you to say, "No, thank you, Mr. Winslow. I'd like to have dinner with you but I've promised Ted I'll be home tonight."

But as Sunny, you, and Mr. Winslow are leaving the store, Sunny whispers, "You should have come with us, you know," before following her father out the door.

She doesn't look back.

HEARTBURN AND HEART PAIN

This could be the title for a country music song.

Taco takeout indigestion.

And stupid, stupid, stupid Ducky.

Asking Ted's advice?

AGAIN?

WHAT WERE YOU THINKING?

First he says, "Maggie's a babe! She's the one

giving you problems? Let me tell you, she's worth it —
even if she does travel with a little brother."

You tell him she's a friend, not a babe.

"She's cute," he says.

"She'll be thrilled you said so," you retort.

He says, "Problems, Ducky?"

This should have been your cue to give up.

But you say Maggie isn't the one giving you
problems, and that you are still having problems with
the other girl, the one you don't like "that way."

You've avoided mentioning Sunny's name. No point in
giving Ted too much information.

You don't want to have to clean up the mess when
his head explodes.

He chuckles. "Ducky the chick magnet," he says.

And continues like that. You should have known he
would say brilliant things like, "Give it spin. Check out
the menu. Drive to the hoop, man."

You say, "Sunny is not a) a car; b) an entree; or c)
a basketball."

You storm out of the family room, leaving Ted
puzzled but unafflicted.

This has taught you, Ducky, a lesson.

Asking advice is not going to help. The only thing
that is going to help is dealing with it yourself.

TOMORROW.

DEFINITELY TOMORROW.

AUG. 29
THE HISTORY OF MY SUNDAY, PART I

So MAGGIE'S OKAY.

YOU ARE RELIEVED THAT ONE THING IN LIFE IS GOING BETTER.

MAGGIE SAID THAT ON THE WAY HOME FROM THE BOOKSTORE, HER FATHER TOLD THEM WHAT HE HAD ALREADY PLANNED. (YOU MIGHT HAVE KNOWN THAT PEOPLE IN CHARGE OF BIG THINGS LIKE MOVIES WOULD GET THINGS DONE. ON THE OTHER HAND, YOU CAN'T HELP BUT NOTICE THAT MR. BLUME SPENT A LOT OF TIME AND EFFORT AVOIDING THE WHOLE SITUATION — AND LEAVING HIS KIDS TO STEW IN IT. GOOD GOING, MR. BLUME.)

BUT YOU DON'T SAY THIS TO MAGGIE, BRILLIANT DUCKY THAT YOU ARE.

MR. BLUME SAYS HE'S ALREADY TALKED TO THE BETTY FORD CENTER, A PLACE WHERE PEOPLE WITH DRUG AND DRINKING PROBLEMS GO TO GET BETTER. THEY ARE WAITING FOR HIM TO BRING MRS. BLUME IN. BUT FIRST THERE'S

GOING TO BE AN "INTERVENTION." HE AND TWO OF MRS. B's
BEST FRIENDS ARE COMING OVER TO CONFRONT MRS. B "IN A
FIRM, CARING WAY" ABOUT HER DRINKING.

MAGGIE AND ZEKE CAN OPT OUT OF THIS PART.

THE SCENE AT THE BLUME HOUSE IS NOT NICE IN A BIG
WAY. (YOU'RE NOT THERE, OF COURSE, BUT MAGGIE'S TOLD
YOU ABOUT IT.) MRS. BLUME IS DRUNK. THE HOUSE IS
TRASHED, ALTHOUGH PILAR HAS BEEN THERE CLEANING UP.
MRS. B DOESN'T EVEN SEEM TO HAVE NOTICED THAT HER
OWN TWO KIDS WERE MISSING. (MAGGIE HAD LEFT A NOTE FOR
PILAR THAT, FORTUNATELY, SURVIVED MRS. B's RAMPAGE.)

EVEN MR. BLUME LOOKS TAKEN ABACK.

MAGGIE AND ZEKE HEAD FOR THE RELATIVE PEACE AND
QUIET OF THEIR ROOMS AS MR. BLUME TRIES TO SETTLE
MRS. BLUME DOWN.

HE SUCCEEDS.

THINGS ARE QUIET. UNTIL THE DOORBELL RINGS.

AND RINGS AGAIN.

AFTER AWHILE, MAGGIE SLIPS OUT ONTO THE STAIR
LANDING IN TIME TO HEAR RACHEL, ONE OF MRS. BLUME's
TWO FRIENDS, SAY FROM THE LIBRARY, "WHY WOULD I MAKE
THIS UP? YOU ARE AN ALCOHOLIC."

"YOU DRINK TOO. YOU WERE LOADED AT THE NEW YEAR'S
PARTY." MRS. BLUME'S VOICE IS OFF THE SCALE.

MAGGIE FEELS ZEKE SIT DOWN NEXT TO HER.

Rachel says, "We're not talking about me. We're talking about you."

"We're not talking about me, we're talking about you," Mrs. B spits back.

Mr. Blume says something Maggie can't quite catch.

Her mother's voice comes through loud and clear, though. She says, "I don't need help! I'm fine. You know what your problem is? You've got too much time on your hands. Take up a hobby. Knitting. Go knit yourself a life."

Maggie is on her feet before she knows it. With Zeke right behind her she goes down the stairs and into the family room.

"Mom, you're a drunk!" Maggie shouts, bursting in.

Mr. B holds up his hand as if to stop Maggie. She remembers what he said about an intervention: caring, firm.

Not nasty. Not angry.

Maggie reins herself in.

"I love you, Mom. We all do. But you are killing yourself. Just like I was killing myself when I wasn't eating. It's a disease and you're going to die if you don't start fighting back."

"Don't drink, Mama," Zeke says. "Don't die."

Mrs. B says, "I'm not sick. I feel fine."

Maggie just looks at her mother. Her eyes are filling with tears but she doesn't turn away.

"It's not true!" Mrs. B shouts. "I can quit anytime I want. I just don't want to."

Mrs. B's other friend, Corrine, puts her hand on Mrs. B's arm. "Listen to your children," she says softly. "Listen to the people who love you most in the world."

Mrs. B falters. "It's not true," she says. And then she says, "I'm sorry." She keeps apologizing. And promising she'll do better.

Mr. B says, "Yes, good. You're going to Betty Ford."

Mrs. B stops apologizing and says, "No! I'm not that bad. The Betty Ford Center is for people who have real problems."

No one says anything. They all just look at Mrs. Blume.

Her face collapses. She wails, "Noooo."

Maggie wants to go to her, tell her it's all right.

Except that it isn't. And Maggie isn't going to pretend it is anymore.

It's Mr. B who says it's over. That it's gone too far. It's gone on too long. Everyone has tried to cope, but they can't anymore. Mrs. B needs help that they can't give.

By now Mrs. B is really crying.

"Anyway," Maggie concludes what she's telling you brightly. "She's left. Gone. On her way to Betty's."

When you ask her how she feels, Maggie says, "Fine."

You don't say anything.

Maggie says, "Okay. Fine, a little. Scared, a lot. Hopeful and afraid to hope. It could all go wrong. I don't want to think about it. I don't want to hope. But maybe... maybe just facing the fact that Mom is an alcoholic will make a difference for all of us."

Aug. 29
History of Ducky's Sunday, Part II

You hang out around the house until midafternoon.

You watch some pretty dumb movies.

You waste time on the Web.

You clean the kitchen.

You give up and go to Sunny's house. But she's not home.

No one is. While you are standing halfway down the front walk, thinking about leaving a note (bad idea), making a few phone calls (not appealing), or driving around aimlessly pretending you are searching for

Sunny (appealing — a good, guilt-free way to waste time, except for the waste of fossil fuel), Dawn shouts your name from next door.

You accept her invitation to enter her casa and go to the mat with baby Gracie.

Gracie laughs at all your jokes. Fortunately, you don't suspect her of having a hidden, terrifying agenda.

As if she has read your mind, Dawn observes that babies have it easy.

"They don't worry about expectations," she says. "They just put it out there. They're happy? They laugh. They're hungry? They cry. No miscommunications. No hurt feelings. And they're willing to forgive you if you make a mistake. So you think they're crying because they want food and you discover they want to be changed. Change them — they're happy, you're happy."

You say, "Yeah."

Ducky the great communicator.

Dawn says, not unexpectedly, given the lead-in: "So, what about you and Sunny? Any chance?"

Just like that, she asks the question.

The two-letter negative is on the tip of your tongue, but you lack the straightforwardness of a mere baby like Gracie.

You say, "Well, uh."

You say, "Sunny's great. I love her, but..."

You say, "I wish I could be different about this."

You finally wind down your extended version of "N" followed by "O."

Gracie is staring at you. Dawn is studying you too.

You pretend Gracie is fascination personified. She agrees and laughs in delight.

Somewhere above you, Dawn says, "It's too bad. But I do understand, Ducky, more than you think. And you know what? Sunny will too. Eventually."

You hope that this is TRUE and that it will happen SOON.

Aug. 29
History of Ducky's Sunday, Part III

P.M. approaching A.M.

You... no, I wish I could fall in love with Sunny.

I do, I do, I really, really do.

But I can't.

Aug. 29
History of Ducky's Sunday, Part IV

You wish you could go to sleep too, don't you, Ducky?
Like Ted the Snore Machine in there.
But you can't.
Not until you've talked to Sunny.

You get up and go into the kitchen. Maybe you'll clean something else: the laundry room, the den.

You forgot you used up all the cleaning supplies on the kitchen.

Aug. 29
History of Ducky's Sunday, Part V

So what are you going to say? If you go with the "just be friends" routine, it's gonna sound like the lame lose-yourself it usually is.

How did "just" get to be attached to the word "friends" anyway?

You've lived a long time without a girlfriend and a pretty good while without anything like a family in residence.

But you could live, oh, ten minutes without friends.

Friends are your family of choice. You get to choose them. That's what so cool about it. And they choose you.

That's true love, if you ask . . . you.

Aug. 29
History of Ducky's Sunday, Part VI

That's it. You're going to sleep even if you have to lie in bed awake for the RESTOFTHENIGHT.

Aug. 30

So you've told Sunny, in a particularly graceful and suave way, that you HAVE to talk to her, as in:

Scene: Bookstore, moments after opening. You emerge from the rest room and there's Sunny.

D: Sunny!

S: Good morning, Ducky.

D: Sunny.

S: [A look]

D: Uh, can we talk?
S: [long pause] Okay. After work.

You are not sure whether you are relieved for
the time to think about it, or whether you just wish it
were over with already.

5:15

Late break. You are sucking back coffee because
when you're nervous, that helps your nerves, right?
You are sitting on a bench behind a tree, like
some spy.
You can see Sunny inside the bookstore as you
skulk.
She is laughing at something her father has said
to a customer (you surmise). Or maybe it's something
the customer said....
Stop this. Off the point.
The point is...
What is the point?
What if Sunny looks at you and says that? "Ducky,
what's the point?"
What if she says, "Let's just be friends."

And that means that she is no longer your friend because there are ways of saying it and other ways of saying it and you don't like the possibility of the way you think she might say it.

You are losing it.

Definitely.

Two more customers just walked in.

Must leap from behind the tree and get back inside to work.

Later

Is this weird, to hang out in your car? To hang out in your car writing in your journal?

Or what?

At least you're not hanging out on a bench. The grocery store parking lot is not so strange. After all, you could just be writing up a grocery list.

Of cleaning supplies.

This is what happened.

You hover around the register as Mr. W closes it out. He looks up, smiles. "Take off," he says. "See you at home, Sunny?"

"Yep," she says. "For dinner."

She takes your hand and leads you out of the store. You are a) grateful for the guidance; and b) PANICKED THAT SHE IS HOLDING YOUR HAND.

Your hand starts to sweat.

Also your neck.

You follow Sunny to your car. She says, "The beach."

So you drive to the beach. Sunny doesn't say anything. She fiddles with the sad excuse you call a car radio.

At the beach, you pull into a deserted end of the lot.

Sunny gets out.

She jumps up onto the hood of your car.

You do the same.

You both stare out at the ocean.

Farther up the beach is the surfers' zone. Farther down is the family spot, where the waves are gentler.

Here it's anything goes.

Someone, you think a young woman, is doing the slow movements of Tai Chi.

Two guys are sitting cross-legged, playing some kind of board game.

A man and a woman with six golden retrievers and a Jack Russell terrier are throwing about a

HUNDRED TENNIS BALLS INTO THE SURF FOR THE DOGS TO RETRIEVE.

YOU DECIDE YOU IDENTIFY WITH ONE OF THE TENNIS BALLS. SMASHED IN THE WAVES. GNASHED IN A DOG'S TEETH.

YOU TAKE A DEEP BREATH TO BEGIN TO RUIN WHAT IS LEFT OF YOUR RELATIONSHIP WITH SUNNY.

SHE BEATS YOU TO IT.

SHE SAYS, "I HATE THIS. I HATE IT, DUCKY."

"YOU DO?" YOU CROAK.

FOR A MOMENT, YOU THINK SHE'S SAID, "I HATE YOU, DUCKY." BUT SHE HASN'T.

NOT YET.

"I DO," SHE SAYS. "I HATE WHAT'S HAPPENING. I HATE THE WAY YOU LOOK SCARED WHENEVER I TALK TO YOU. I HATE THE WAY YOU STAND THERE BUT SORT OF BACK UP, LIKE WITH YOUR EYES, YOU KNOW? DETACH. DISTANCE YOURSELF. I HATE MYSELF FOR KISSING YOU, BECAUSE I SHOULD HAVE KNOWN SOMETHING LIKE THIS WOULD HAPPEN. IF I COULD UNKISS YOU, I WOULD. TOTALLY. IN A HEARTBEAT."

"OH," YOU SAY.

ONE OF THE RETRIEVERS HAS MANAGED TO PUT THREE BALLS INTO ITS MOUTH. IT IS TRYING TO PICK UP A FOURTH, BUT SO FAR, NO LUCK.

SUNNY ELBOWS YOU. "YOUR TURN," SHE SAYS.

"YOU'D UNKISS ME?" YOU SAY. "THAT'S NOT VERY FLATTERING."

"Ducky," she says in a warning voice.

"Yeah," you say. And then, words come, more or less. You tell her how completely miserable you've been. That you can't sleep. That it's not her fault and you're sorry about the scared look, but it wasn't fear of what she would do, it was fear of your own reaction. You believed that if you reacted wrong, you would scorch her feelings and ruin your friendship and it's the one thing in the whole wide world you couldn't stand. You love Sunny way too much and have for way too long to feel any differently, to feel in love. You don't know why, but it's not there. It's something just as strong, maybe stronger. You say, "Some people are meant to be just boyfriend and girlfriend. But others are meant to be best friends."

"Best friends," says Sunny, seeming to perk up.

"Nah."

"You don't wanna be my best friend?" you ask, pretending you're hurt.

"You mean it?" she asks.

"Forever and always," you say.

Sunny sighs and leans against you for a minute. You feel comfortable and happy and you put your arm around her and you sit there, pondering love and life and golden retrievers and Jack Russells.

Then Sunny straightens. "Don't get all mush-

BRAINED ON ME," SHE SAYS. "THAT'S PROBABLY WHY I KISSED YOU IN THE FIRST PLACE — THE MUSH FACTOR OF SUMMER."

"AND I THOUGHT IT WAS MY UNIQUE SENSE OF STYLE," YOU JOKE BACK.

SUNNY ROLLS HER EYES. "I'LL GIVE YOU UNIQUE," SHE SAYS.

YOU LAUGH. "YOU'RE THE ONE WHO DREAMS OF PERSONALIZED BOWLING SHIRTS," YOU SAY.

AND SUNNY LAUGHS.

IT FEELS SO GOOD.

BEST FRIENDS.

LATER

YOU ARE NO LONGER HANGING OUT IN THE PARKING LOT OF THE GROCERY STORE.

YOU ACTUALLY WENT IN AND BOUGHT CLEANING SUPPLIES.

HOWEVER, YOU NO LONGER FEEL THE NEED TO KEEP BUSY IN A PRODUCTIVE WAY.

YOU ARE NOW WATCHING A BAD FLICK, IN WHICH A MONSTER FROM OUTER SPACE IS TAKING OVER A MOVIE SET.

YOU ARE DEBATING THE DIFFERENCE BETWEEN SCIENCE FICTION AND HORROR.

YOU WONDER WHY TEACHERS NEVER GIVE THESE

QUESTIONS AS ASSIGNMENTS: DESCRIBE YOUR SUMMER VACATION IN TERMS OF: A) A HORROR MOVIE OR B) A SCIENCE FICTION FLICK.

You WOULD LIKE TO POINT OUT THAT SUMMER VACATIONS EXIST ONLY IN THE MINDS OF CHILDREN AND TEACHERS. You PERSONALLY HAVE HAD FAR TOO MUCH WORK TO DO THIS SUMMER.

And you don't MEAN THE BOOKSTORE.

The MOVIE WILL HAVE A HAPPY ENDING. The BAD GUY WILL GET TURNED INTO MONSTER MASH.

You ARE ROOTING FOR THE MONSTER TO GO ON TO BECOME A MOVIE STAR AND THEN PRESIDENT OF THE United States, JUST LIKE Ronald Reagan!!!

Does your SUMMER HAVE A HAPPY ENDING?

Hard TO SAY. Not DEFINITE. No SCREEN KISS FADE TO CREDITS.

As FIRST KISSES GO, FOR EXAMPLE (you ARE NOT COUNTING THAT TIME IN THIRD GRADE) THIS WAS FAIRLY UNSUCCESSFUL. You WILL NEED MORE LIP-LOCK LEARNING.

Later.

And NOT WITH Sunny.

Some THINGS ARE LIKE THAT. Some THINGS END, ROLL THE CREDITS, EVERYBODY LIVES HAPPILY EVER AFTER. You BELIEVE THIS IS TRUE EVEN IN REAL LIFE.

Sometimes.

Occasionally.

But you, Duckster, know that you are not John Wayne. You are not that kind of hero and you don't get that kind of ending, at least not this time.

You and Sunny have this kind of ending: Your friendship endured. Maybe it will be stronger, better.

Or maybe not.

Meanwhile, you've both just agreed that enough has been said, and no more needs to be done. Time to let it go. Time to let it slide.

It's like a piece of your back story. Maybe someday you'll look back and laugh.

Or not.

Only time will tell.

You just have to go with that.

Sept. 4
9:00 A.M.
School Looms

Like, practically tomorrow, if you don't count Sunday.

Why wouldn't you count Sunday?

Don't get into religion now, Ducky.

It makes people uncomfortable. Even more uncomfortable than talking about sex.

You don't feel comfortable with either subject, so moving right along....

Busy, busy, like, you know, busy.

Let's count Saturday, anyway. You know how you feel about Saturday.

In just a few hours you, Ducky, will be the Saturday-night party animal.

Why yes. You are having a party. At your house. With your parents' long-distance permission.

When you talked to them, you listened while they discussed the Greek influence in Roman mosaics and the confluence of cultural cross-fertilization.

You thought this sounded like either sex or gardening but you had sense enough to keep your mouth shut. You heard the strangled sound Ted made and knew he was trying not to laugh.

Then your mother mentioned the possibility that she and your father might try a cooking class vacation.

"Sounds great, Mom," Ted said in his "Sincerely Your Son, Ted" voice.

"Mmm," you said. "Speaking of cooking, Mom, I'm thinking of cooking up a back-to-school get-together for my friends."

"How nice," said she.

"What sort of party?" asked your father, not to be fooled for an instant by soft words and creative segues.

"Just a few friends," you say.

"Define a few," your father says.

"Eight to twelve."

In fact, if you are able to muster twelve friends, you've got friends you didn't know you had, but you don't want to explore that with your parents or Ted.

"That sounds nice," your mother says, heading off further interrogation. "You'll be there, won't you, Ted?"

"Count on me," Ted says heartily, in that same voice.

"I thought we could cook out," you let slip, before realizing you are venturing into the land of too much information. Your mother says, "Be careful. Wear oven mitts."

Your father says, "Use the fire-starting chimney, NOT lighter fluid."

"I know," you say. Then you let him tell you about the dangers of lighter fluid and how people have crisped themselves squirting it into open flames.

Then you realize that talking about cooking out has diverted them from their cross-examination mode and you say, "Well, maybe we'll just do pizza or something."

Relieved, your father says, heartily (and sounding disconcertingly Ted-like), "Well, that's fine, then. That's great."

You get off the phone before they can think of any more questions or dispense any more advice.

You think about reassuring them that you won't burn down the house, but you decide against it.

Smart boy, that Ducky.

Okay, okay, you haven't written all week.

Oh, sure, you can find time to write about all the STUFF, the DIRE COMPLICATIONS, the EXTREME DIFFICULTIES of your life. Those you chronicle faithfully.

After all, that's what your journal is about, isn't it? Problems. Previously, mostly other people's problems.

So is this progress? That you have spent days, weeks, hours, hand-cramping aeons worrying about and writing about a problem of your own? To the point of seeming self-centered?

Who knows?

Or maybe you prefer the problems of other people. Is that sick, or what? But you can offer other people:

Sympathy, or

Advice, or

Help.

With your own life, you realize that sympathy is nice, advice may or may not be useful depending on the source, and help?

Help is not something that necessarily fixes the problem.

In the end,

YOU ARE ON YOUR OWN.

As if you didn't know that already.

But enough of this obsession with your problems, Christopher.

Let's show this journal the fun side of your life.

As in: the party that will soon start.

As in: happy endings (or at least, a few pretty good moments, you hope).

Uh-oh. Big crash in the house. Better check it out.

THE STORY OF TED,
YOUR BROTHER
THE CRASH TEST DUMMY

So this is the sitcom moment that meets your eyes as you scope out what caused the minor earthquake somewhere in your house.

Your brother is entangled, in a bad way, with the vacuum cleaner.

Also a chair, some of a small rug (which is in the vacuum cleaner nozzle), and a former vase of flowers.

The vacuum is sucking that rug. Ted is kicking at the vacuum. The cord of the vacuum is wrapped around one of the chair legs.

D: Ted, I don't think you should be doing that with the vacuum.

T: GET THIS OFF ME.

D: But how do you really feel?

T: I'm warning you, Christopher.

D: I feel your pain!

T: (unprintable expressions of frustration and vacuum rage)

So you take pity on the guy, walk over, and pull the plug.

The vacuum spits out the rug.

You unwrap Ted from its embrace.

You say, "Ted? What were you doing?"

Ted stands up and glares. Then he rocks your

WORLD. HE SAYS, "WELL, SINCE YOU'RE HAVING A PARTY TONIGHT, I THOUGHT I'D MAYBE CLEAN UP A LITTLE."

YOU GRAB THE CHAIR, RIGHT IT, AND COLLAPSE INTO IT.

TED SAYS, "WHAT?"

YOU REJECT JOKES AS INAPPROPRIATE. ALSO, YOU DON'T WANT TO DISCOURAGE TED. YOU SETTLE FOR, "OKAY. WHAT HAPPENED?"

TED SHRUGS. "I DON'T KNOW. I WAS VACUUMING. THEN IT GOT THE RUG. SO I STOOD ON THE OTHER END OF THE RUG TO HOLD IT DOWN AND TRIED TO YANK IT OUT. I GUESS I PULLED THE RUG OUT FROM UNDER ME. I'M NOT SURE HOW THE CHAIR GOT KNOCKED OVER. OR THE FLOWERS."

"IT COULD HAPPEN TO ANYONE." YOU ARE TRYING SO HARD NOT TO LAUGH AND IT IS KILLING YOU.

TED SAYS, "YEAH. WELL, THANKS FOR THE HELP. I GUESS I'LL FINISH UP IN HERE AND, UH, HEAD OUT. YOU NEED ANYTHING FOR TONIGHT?"

"GOT IT COVERED," YOU ASSURE HIM. "BUT THANKS."

"ANYTIME," HE SAYS.

HE WAITS UNTIL YOU LEAVE TO PLUG IN THE VACUUM AGAIN. YOU RESOLVE THAT NO MATTER WHAT HAPPENS, YOU WILL NOT GO DOWN TO THE FAMILY ROOM AGAIN.

YOU HOPE TED CAN'T HEAR YOU LAUGHING IN YOUR ROOM OVER THE SOUND OF THE VACUUM.

MAYBE YOU SHOULD DO A LITTLE CLEANING TOO. OF

course, you've been trying to impose order on chaos all week, so the task ahead is not too huge.

You hope.

A Midparty
Journal Moment

You almost wore the old bowling shirt you wore when you had that unfortunate kiss incident with Sunny.

But you decided against it. Too symbolic or something.

Sunny is not wearing a bowling shirt either. She still hasn't found one with her name on it. She says she's wearing something even more retro: an old gym shirt.

To which Maggie says, "Yuck."

Sunny says, "It's clean."

The name embroidered over the pocket is "Elaine." It has snap buttons and no collar.

You like the look. Even with someone else's name over the pocket. You tell her so.

She says, "It has shorts to go with it. But I couldn't quite see it."

"The skirt is better," you agree.

Ted is upstairs with some buds, watching movies in his room. He comes out from time to time. His excuse is a trip to the refrigerator for more stomach supplies, but you realize he is also keeping an eye on the party.

Does he expect it to turn into some kind of major Ted-style blowout?

He's in for a disappointment.

You made it very clear that you did not want your friends telling everyone about a party in a parent-free house.

You like not having your parents around when you throw a party. You do not like being responsible for what would be left of the house after word got out that you were having a party and no adults were around to spoil the fun.... Fun like puking in the plants and dancing on the tables and driving cars across the lawn and...

Gotta go.

YAWNS.

LATER

So it was a good party, if you do say so yourself.

You ate junk food and played Frisbee in the backyard using a glow-in-the-dark Frisbee.

Amalia and Brendan seem to be getting along better; she no longer moves away when he puts his arm around her.

At the same time, you suspect that he's being careful not to be too pushy.

It's possible that once Amalia reached for Brendan's hand for a moment.

You call a time-out from Frisbee and you go in to make pizzas (edible Frisbees, Sunny points out).

Sunny takes charge, organizing the ingredients, wrapping people in aprons made out of towels and tablecloths.

Maggie gets into rolling out the pizza dough on the kitchen table. "We're going for the thin crust," she tells everybody. "You can taste the flavors better that way."

"Chef Maggie," Dawn teases her and Maggie smiles.

Sunny puts you in charge of "Vegetables and Sharp

OBJECTS." That means you have to chop up onions and peppers and even the pitted olives.

You sit across from Maggie and she talks about her mom a little. How she's in treatment. How the doctors have high hopes. How she and Zeke visited her briefly and how different she already was. "Like she knows she has to do this," Maggie says. "Like it's important to her."

"Good," you say.

"Yeah," Maggie says. "It is."

Then she puts the dough in the pizza pan (you are a genius — you remembered to buy pizza pans when you bought the dough) and starts on another.

When the pizzas are done, you pizza out.

You go back outside, but only Amalia and Brendan have the energy to throw the Frisbee around.

You sprawl in the grass. Sunny is next to you. She says, "I figure we let everybody have ice-cream sundaes in about half an hour."

"At least." Dawn, who is propped against a tree, groans. "I didn't know I could eat so much pizza. How am I going to eat ice-cream sundaes?"

Maggie says, "With a spoon!" and cracks up like a little kid.

You hear Sunny laughing and you turn. In the half-dark, she smiles at you. You smile back and relax.

You and Sunny are still a team. A good team. In spite of all the drama of the past few weeks.

After awhile, you make ice-cream sundaes.

Dawn glances up as Sunny takes charge of that too. She smiles, relieved.

She's glad you and Sunny are still friends.

Glad, like you, that your friendship survived this bad time.

You go outside to wave good night when everyone leaves. Sunny gives your hand a squeeze. "Not bad, Ducky. Just what we needed."

"Ice cream, pizza, and friends," Maggie adds.

Brendan says, "Here's to it, especially the friends part."

"Especially," Maggie echoes.

"And here's to this year and everything amazing that is going to happen," Dawn adds.

"That too," Amalia agrees.

And then they are gone.

You stand on the front walk until they are gone. Then you stand there some more.

You look up at the stars.

If you wished on a star, you'd wish for friends exactly like these.

You, Christopher, are one lucky Duck.

Ann M. Martin

About the Author

ANN MATTHEWS MARTIN was born on August 12, 1955. She grew up in Princeton, NJ, with her parents and her younger sister, Jane.

Although Anne used to be a teacher and then an editor of children's books, she's now a full-time writer. She gets the ideas for her books from many different places. Some are based on personal experiences. Others are based on childhood memories and feelings. Many are written about contemporary problems or events.

All of Ann's characters are made up. But some of her characters are based on real people. Sometimes Anne names her characters after people she knows; other times she chooses names she likes.

In addition to California Diaries, Ann Martin has written many other books, including the Baby-sitters Club series. She has written twelve novels for young people, including *Missing Since Monday, With You or Without You, Slam Book,* and *Just a Summer Romance.*

Ann M. Martin does not live in California, though she does visit frequently. She lives in New York with her cats, Gussie, Woody, and Willy, and her dog, Sadie. Her hobbies are reading, sewing, and needlework — especially making clothes for children.